HIDING TOADS

by Suzanne Paul Dell'Oro

Pull Ahead Books

Lerner Publications Company • Minneapolis

Lerner Publications Company
A Division of the Lerner Publishing Group
241 First Avenue North
Minneapolis, MN 55401

Website address: www.lernerbooks.com

Curriculum Development Director: Nancy M. Campbell

Words in *italic type* are explained in a glossary
on page 30.

Library of Congress Cataloging-in-Publication Data

Dell'Oro, Suzanne Paul.
    Hiding toads / by Suzanne Paul Dell'Oro.
       p. cm. — (Pull ahead books)
    Includes index.
    Summary: Introduces the physical characteristics,
behavior, habitats, and life cycle of North American toads.
    ISBN 0-8225-3626-9 (hc. : alk. paper). —
    ISBN 0-8225-3630-7 (pbk. : alk. paper)
    1. Toads—Juvenile literature. [1. Toads.] I. Title.
II. Series.
QL668.E227D465 1999
597.8'7'097—dc21   98–49380

Manufactured in the United States of America
1 2 3 4 5 6 – JR – 04 03 02 01 00 99

Where is the animal
hiding in this picture?

This is a toad. Toads are animals that hide a lot.

They hide in the woods.

They hide near your house.

They hide in many cool, wet places. Why do toads hide?

Hiding helps toads stay alive.

A toad is a kind of animal called an *ectotherm.*

When the air around an ectotherm gets cold, its body gets cold, too.

During very cold weather, toads hide underground to stay warm.

Toads also hide from the hot sun.
Sunshine can dry out their skin.

Toads must keep their skin wet.

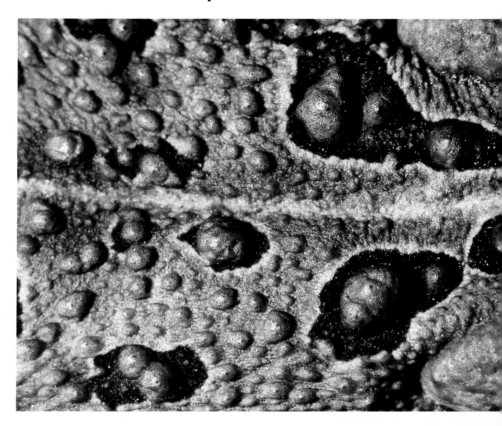

Toads can breathe through
their bumpy skin if it is wet.

Toads can
also drink
water
through
their skin.

Many toads come out at night.
Do you know why?

Night is cooler and wetter than day. Night is dark, too.

It is easy to hide from other animals in the dark.

Toads are *carnivores.* Carnivores
are animals that eat other animals.

Hiding helps toads catch
the animals they eat.

Toads move too slowly to chase fast animals like crickets or moths.

A toad sits still and waits quietly. What is it waiting for?

Surprise!
This toad catches a caterpillar.

The caterpillar did not notice
the toad and came too close.

Hiding also helps toads stay safe
from animals that might eat them.

This toad is making itself flat
to look like a rock.

If hiding does not work,
toads stay safe in other ways.

This toad is playing dead. Most
animals will not eat dead things.

This toad is dripping poison
from its skin.

This toad is puffing itself up
so a snake cannot swallow it.

This toad is jumping
to get away from something.

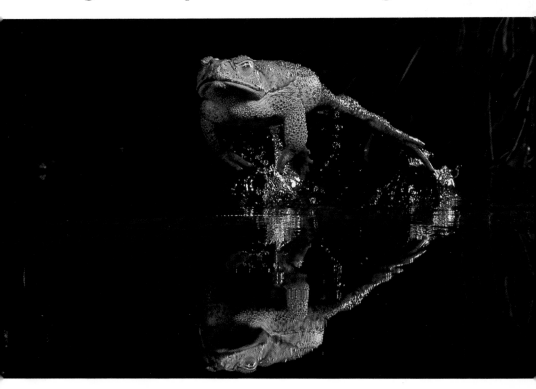

Long, strong back legs help
the toad jump fast and far.

Swimming is a good way
to get away, too.

Toads live part of their lives
in water and part on land.

Animals that live this way
are called *amphibians*.

Toads start life in water.
Baby toads come from eggs.

Mother toads lay eggs in long
strings covered with slimy jelly.

Baby toads called *tadpoles*
come out of the eggs.

Tadpoles live underwater like fish.
Tadpoles eat plants.

This is an older tadpole. How
is it different from a young one?

As a tadpole gets older, it grows
two eyes and two back legs.

Then it grows two front legs. Its
tail shrinks as its body gets bigger.

It starts eating animals
instead of plants.

Then it leaves the water. It is not a tadpole anymore. It is a tiny toad.

Toads live in many places.
They hide from many things.

They even hide from you!

KEY:

⬜ shows
where
toads live

N ↑

Find your state or province on this map.
Do toads live near you?

Parts of a Toad's Body

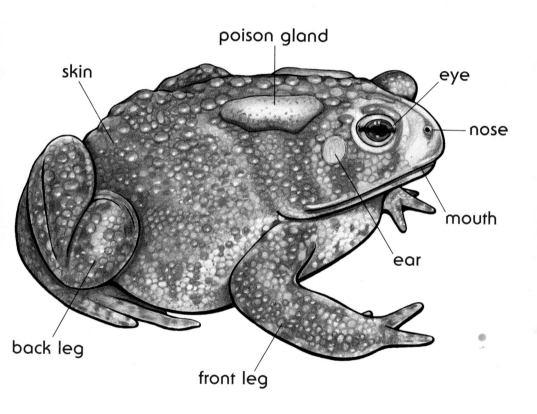

poison gland

skin

eye

nose

mouth

ear

back leg

front leg

Glossary

amphibians: animals that have slimy skin and usually spend part of their lives in water and part on land. (Frogs, toads, and salamanders are amphibians.)

carnivores: animals that eat other animals

ectotherm: an animal whose body heat changes to match the warmth or cold around it

tadpoles: baby toads

Hunt and Find

- toads **eating** on pages 12, 14
- toad **eggs** on page 22
- toads **hiding underground** on pages 7–8
- a **jumping** toad on page 19
- toad **poison** on page 17
- **tadpoles** on pages 23–25

The publisher wishes to extend special thanks to our **series consultant,** Sharyn Fenwick. An elementary science-math specialist, Mrs. Fenwick was the recipient of the National Science Teachers Association 1991 Distinguished Teaching Award. In 1992, representing the state of Minnesota at the elementary level, she received the Presidential Award for Excellence in Math and Science Teaching.

About the Author

Suzanne Paul Dell'Oro lives in Minneapolis, Minnesota, with her husband, their three children, and the family cat. She has liked toads all her life. When she was young, she used to catch live bugs to feed her pet toad, Toby. Suzanne writes about many different subjects, and she helped write *Sneaky Salamanders* for Lerner's Pull Ahead series.

Photo Acknowledgments

The photographs in this book are reproduced through the courtesy of: © W. Banaszewski/Visuals Unlimited (VU), page 22; © Bill Beatty/VU, page 14; © Robert Clay/VU, page 5; © David F. Clobes, pages 11, 16; © Wally Eberhart/VU, page 3; © John Gerlach/VU, pages 8, 15, 20; © Dwight R. Kuhn, page 9; © Joe McDonald/VU, pages 12, 19; © Gary Meslaros/VU, page 10; © Nada Pecnik/VU, page 6; © David T. Roberts/Nature's Images Inc. (NII), page 26; © David M. Schleser/NII, pages 13, 17, 24, 25, 27; © John Serrao/VU, page 18; © A. B. Sheldon, front cover, page 7; © Alan D. St. John, back cover, pages 21, 31; © Roger Treadwell/VU, page 23; © Garry Walter/VU, page 4.